Magical Mayhem

Part Eleven
To Prevent Good Luck

Emily Martha Sorensen

Also by Emily Martha Sorensen

Wicked Witches of Restva:
Black Magic Academy
White Magic Academy

The End in the Beginning:
The Keeper and the Rulership
The Fires of the Rulership
The Magic or the Rulership

Fairy Senses:
Fairy Eyeglasses
Fairy Compass
Fairy Earmuffs
Fairy Barometer
Fairy Pox
Fairy Slippers
Fairy Lunchbox
Fairy Icepack
Fairy Stopwatch
Fairy Toothbrush
Fairy Perfume
Fairy Crown

Dragon Eggs:
Dragon's Egg
Dragon's Hope
Dragon's First Christmas
Dragon's Fire
Dragon's Song
Dragon's First Valentine

Comics:
A Magical Roommate
To Prevent World Peace

The Numbers Just Keep
Getting Bigger:
*Twenty-Four Potential
Children of Prophecy*

Trilogy of a Teenage Werevulture:
Trials of a Teenage Werevulture
Trifles of a Teenage Werevulture

Weredodo Cozy Mysteries:
Weredodo Sleuth

Not Quite a Harem:
Not Quite a Curse

Magical Mayhem:
To Prevent World Peace
To Prevent Chic Costumes
To Prevent Clear Paths
To Prevent Smart Choices
To Prevent Warm Welcomes
To Prevent Cute Mascots
To Prevent First Place (prologue)
To Prevent Fresh Starts
To Prevent New Allies
To Prevent Best Friends

Short Story Collections:
Worlds of Wonder
Magic and Mischief
Tales of Tie-Ins

Picture Books:
Tabby, Tabby, Burning Bright

To Prevent Good Luck

http://www.emilymarthasorensen.com

To Frederik Vendelin,

longtime fan of the comic,
reader of my other books,
and Patreon supporter.

Chapter 1
The Luck

Veils of cigarette smoke drifted across the room. Dice were rolled, cards were shuffled, wheels were spun, and Felix placed a hand on his daughter's shoulder.

"This is my underaged daughter, Amy Marin," he bragged to a casino employee walking by him. "She's my good luck charm. Aren't you, Amy?"

The girl's voice was soft. "Yes, Daddy."

The casino employee walked past without noticing either his comment or his daughter's presence.

Felix guffawed in amusement. Children weren't allowed in casinos, and magical girls *certainly* weren't, but the two of them had been clever enough to figure out a way around it.

Namely, Amy's focus item, a four-leafed clover that she had found and picked years ago and turned into a focus item so that it wouldn't wither, gave her permanent good luck whenever she was holding it, even if she wasn't transformed.

Because it was a focus item, it could never be taken from her, and she could never lose it.

Unfortunately, that luck only worked on her; she couldn't give it away or transfer it, no matter how convenient it would have been for Felix to be able to borrow it.

But that was why she had her other power.

"Hey, hey! Look at my eleven-year-old daughter! She's standing right here! That's against casino rules, right?" Felix asked one of the other gamblers at his table, grinning broadly.

The man rolled his dice and cursed loudly at having lost his money.

Felix chortled. He loved testing the limits of his daughter's good luck. So far, only ten people out of all the hundreds he'd pointed her out to had paid attention to her presence, and only two had cared enough to insist that she leave.

Oh, sure, a few other sharp-eyed, shrewd people had noticed on their own and kicked the two of them out. Luck was luck, after all, not a guarantee. But the odds were always in their favor, and there were always more casinos to go to.

"Can we leave and get dinner now?" Amy asked nervously. She never seemed to like it when he deliberately pointed her out to other people. The girl had no sense of fun.

"After I win," Felix shrugged. "Speaking of which, my luck's been bad tonight. Blow on these for me."

Amy's head lowered. ". . . Yes, Daddy."

She took the dice from his hand and left the room, walking past the bouncers at the exit just as they were eyeing a scantily clad woman on her way in.

Felix lit a cigarette, chortling. He loved the way her powers worked. They were the best team ever.

And to think that his ex-wife had left them. What had the woman been thinking?

Amy Marin was tired of this. She wanted her father to stop gambling. She wanted to live a normal life, instead of jumping from one wild risk to another. And she definitely didn't want to be on a gambling cruise ship, where she got seasick every minute unless she held on to her four-leaf clover.

And yet, here they were, spending all of the money Daddy had won at his last major horsetrack victory, instead of saving any of it to pay their rent for the next six months.

She never got any say in how they spent their money, even though she was responsible for most of it coming in.

But she didn't dare stop.

Amy set the dice on the floor, put her focus item next to it, raised her arms above her head with her fingers splayed outward, and whispered, "Marina Amethyst!"

The four-leaf clover burrowed into the ground, growing roots and stem and leaves and bud in seconds.

The bud unfurled and released itself from its stem, dancing before her. It was an enormous four-leaf clover, exactly the same as the focus item it had grown from, only a hundred times larger.

Amy hopped through the enormous four-leaf clover. As she passed through, it transformed her white T-shirt with blue sleeves and her jeans with flower pockets into a pale green dress and forest green stockings.

A four-leaf clover blossomed out of her hair, and another appeared on her dress. Then the enormous clover behind her poofed into a wisp of steam and vanished.

When she detransformed later, the clover would reappear, and the whole thing would happen again in reverse.

Taking a deep breath, Amy looked down at the dice regretfully.

She didn't like using her power. The power had been his idea, and she didn't think it was very fair, but there was nothing she could do about it. When Daddy wanted her to use her power, she used her power. There was no other way to make sure he'd win.

Amy picked up the dice, tossed them in the air, and blew vigorously.

The dice spun through the air in a brief maelstrom of magic. Then they twirled and fell to the ground, showing a five and a six.

Those weren't special numbers. Just random. The dice weren't lucky yet.

It was time to make them lucky.

Amy scooped the dice up, put them in a pocket of her skirt, and headed upstairs to the deck.

Lots of strangers were wandering around, which was good. It wasn't good when she had only a few people to pull from.

Amy walked silently across the deck, passing dozens of people, noticed by no one, sometimes affecting them and sometimes not.

A woman leaned over the side of the ship, trying to take a picture of something, then dropped her camera, which landed below with a splash.

"Noooooo! I dropped it!" she wailed.

A man tripped and stumbled, slamming his hand against a wall at an awkward angle as he tried to catch himself.

Another man with short hair dropped a bottle of wine he was carrying, which shattered into tiny fragments all over the deck.

A woman's deck chair collapsed underneath her.

A man who was trying to flirt with a woman got slapped in the face.

This was the cost of Amy's power.

Amy didn't believe luck could come from nowhere. Everything that was lucky had a cost.

A four-leaf clover was the luckiest thing in the world because clovers sucked up luck, and when they had enough, they grew a four-leaf clover. It was like a battery. It would someday run out, but as long as you kept it fresh, it could last for a really long time.

A rabbit's foot was lucky because the rabbit had had such bad luck to get caught and killed that the feet held all the good luck left over that the rabbit hadn't been able to use.

A penny you found was lucky because the person who had dropped it had been unlucky to lose it.

A horseshoe was lucky because it sucked in luck like a magnet, but only if you kept it rightside up. If you held it upside down with the ends pointing downward, it would suck in bad luck, and the only way to get rid of that was to turn it rightside up again.

Ladders were unlucky if you walked under them because they were lucky for the people on top of them. That was why the people on top of them didn't fall off more often.

Black cats were unlucky because they stole everyone else's luck. That was why they were so good at killing everything.

It was also why cats were always lucky about landing on their feet and having nine lives.

So meeting stray cats was always unlucky. Owning cats was sometimes lucky, though, because if cats liked you, they might share some of their luck with you.

Mirrors were the most unlucky thing in the world. They sucked up bad luck and stored it, so if you broke them, all the bad luck leaked into you.

Amy knew that because she had broken the bathroom mirror on the same day Mummy had left.

Not even finding a four-leaf clover four days later had given her enough luck to make Mummy come back. Or enough luck to be able to convince Daddy to stop gambling.

Everything bad that had happened was because of the mirror.

That was why she had to help Daddy, even though she didn't like to. Everything was her fault in the first place.

But the four-leaf clover did help her in all sorts of little ways. When she didn't want to be noticed, she usually wasn't. When Daddy gambled away all his money and they had nothing to buy dinner with, she would find coins or chips or even bills on the floor that others had dropped. When they had to sleep outside because they had no money for a hotel, it never rained.

But she couldn't share that luck with somebody else, and all the luck in the world wouldn't make the employees at a casino ignore her if she tried to gamble for Daddy. Besides, he didn't want her to do it for him. He wanted to do it because he thought it was fun.

If only he didn't, maybe they would still be living a normal life and Amy could be going to school like everyone else her age.

Maybe she would even have friends instead of having to use her good luck to make sure nobody noticed she existed.

Breaking a mirror caused the worst luck in the world.

Having made a circuit of the deck, Amy headed down the stairs back to the casino. She didn't want to walk past the same people again. She was scared of what would happen to them if their luck got too bad. Once she'd seen a man lose a million dollars in one spin of a roulette wheel after she'd taken his luck twice in the same night for Daddy.

She walked through the entrance, unseen by one of the bouncers because he was yawning while the other's view was blocked by a fat man entering at the same time as her.

She walked as quickly as possible across the casino floor, but not quickly enough to avoid hearing a trail of losing streaks in her wake.

"Ooh! Lost again!"

"No! No! NO! I said SEVEN! NO!"

"Please! Just loan me some chips! I know I'll win the next one! Please!"

"Sir, I think you've lost enough for one night."

Reaching her father, Amy silently slipped the dice into his hand. He smirked and patted her on the head. Then he tucked the dice in his pocket and headed over to a game of blackjack.

Amy turned and left. He wouldn't need her any more tonight, and it was always best if she wasn't near him while he was lucky, since that might make more people suspicious.

Having given the dice away, she was no longer a jinx, so she could stay in one place for awhile. She thought maybe she'd go to their room and read for awhile. There was a series about a ballet boarding school and horses that she loved.

"Don't you feel guilty?" a voice said from behind her. "Stealing people's luck to help your dad cheat at gambling?"

Amy stiffened. It was a woman's voice, which meant it probably wasn't a bouncer, but it might be a dealer or another employee of the casino. Were they about to get kicked off the gambling cruise?

"I've never done anything like that," Amy said quickly, walking away without looking behind her. Maybe the stranger would let her escape. "I wouldn't even know how to."

"Oh, puh-lease." There was a derisive snort. "You have a pair of magical dice that you transfer people's luck into and give them to your father. Then he wins just often enough to leave with at least slightly more money than he started out with, only significantly more if it won't make the casino owner suspicious. And your magical girl name is Marina Amethyst."

Amy panicked. How did she know all that?!

"So answer my question," the woman said sardonically from behind her. "Don't you feel guilty?"

Amy hung her head, her blurry gazed fixed on the floor. "I . . . I have no choice. Before I started helping him, Daddy lost everything. Our house . . . Our car . . . Mummy . . ."

She got a sarcastic retort. "Have you considered asking him to *stop?*"

Amy's head snapped up. She stared at the stairs in front of her furiously. "Of course I have! I've begged him! Do you think he listened to me?!"

"So instead, you're enabling his addiction? *Great* choice there."

At last, Amy spun around to face her accuser, tears in her eyes. "What would you have me do?! Let Daddy gamble us into starving again?! I'm eleven!! I can't take care of myself!"

She stopped abruptly, taking in the appearance of the woman behind her.

She was dressed in black, with buckles all over her outfit. Her arms were folded, and she projected an aura of menace. Her age was probably somewhere between fourteen and thirty. Amy wasn't very good at guessing ages.

Amy gulped, suddenly afraid. "You're a villain, aren't you?"

The woman shrugged, her arms still folded. "I do fight corrupt magical girls. So, technically, yes. But I'd rather you not be one of them."

"Are you here to blackmail me?" Amy asked in a very small voice. That would be better than the other possibility, which was that the woman was here to attack her.

"No." The woman snorted. "I've got a teammate who uses her power to cheat on the stock market. We're good for money. I really don't care what you're using the luck for. What I care about is that you're stealing it from other people. That has to stop."

Amy felt panicked butterflies in her stomach. "But I *can't* stop! Daddy needs me!"

"What he needs is a good punch in the face, if you ask me. Corrupting the powers of his Sonnenkinder daughter just to feed his addiction and greed. How disgusting is that?"

"I'm not corrupt, and things aren't going to change!" Amy screamed, clenching her fists and spinning away to face the other direction. "Just leave me alone!"

"Fine." There was the sound of footsteps walking away.

"Fine . . . ?" Amy repeated slowly, turning around.

The woman was walking towards the door to the casino.

"Sure." The woman glanced over her shoulder. "If you won't stop your dad, I'll do it myself."

Amy gasped. "Wh-what are you going to do?!"

"Stop him," the woman in black shrugged. "Duh."

Panicked, Amy raced after her, but the woman vanished in a cloud of sparkles.

Amy looked around frantically.

What was going on?

What was the villain going to do to Daddy?

Since the casino's magic detector would definitely have noticed the teleporting, Kendra didn't waste any time. She teleported straight to the office of the casino manager.

The man jumped to his feet. "Magical girls aren't allowed on the premises!" he roared, pushing a button on his desk.

Kendra took a seat in the chair across from his desk, crossing her legs. "I'm not a magical girl. I'm a villain. I figured you'd want to know which of your patrons is cheating by having a magical girl help him. If you don't want to, though . . ." She shrugged.

Three men in armor with machine guns burst into the room.

The manager held up his hand, eyes wary. He looked at Kendra. "Go on."

"The man's name is Felix Davidson," Kendra said carelessly, waving her hand. "His eleven-year-old daughter has luck magic you can't detect."

"We can detect all magic," the man growled.

"Either you're breaking the law or that's a lie," Kendra said, rolling her eyes. "You're only allowed to have one magic detector by law, and it can't screen for everything, only luck magic."

The man's fists clenched.

"And because you only have one, and it has to cover such a wide area," Kendra said casually, "it can't detect all luck magic, only luck magic over a certain threshold."

The man's veins looked like they were about to burst through his forehead.

Kendra smirked. The limitations of magic detectors were considered proprietary or sometimes even classified information, but the Wings of Justice had been briefed on those details by their FBI handler during their stint as FBI aides. It had been necessary for a mission to capture their arch-nemesis while he was staying at a casino hotel.

"The detector's very sensitive to fluctuations in luck, caused by magic or otherwise," the man said in a tight voice.

"Yeah, but that's just it," Kendra said, keeping a sharp corner of her eye on the machine guns aimed at her while pretending they were of no interest to her at all. "She doesn't *create* luck, unlike most luck-based magical girls. She draws tiny portions of it from her focus item or steals larger portions from other people. There's no change in the ambient luck around her."

The man behind the desk gave her a stony look. One of his fingers twitched.

Kendra instantly teleported out before one of the guns fired.

She landed sprawled on Chronos's lap, sending her boss's crochet hook flying across the room.

"Hi, oracle," Kendra said, hopping off. "Thanks for being a cushion. What's the future like now?"

Chronos gave her a sour look and tried to lean over to pick up her crochet hook, which had rolled several feet away. She finally had to get up to retrieve it.

"It looks a little better," Chronos said at last, settling back into her chair and dropping a mess of loops onto her lap. Kendra wasn't sure what crocheting was supposed to look like, but she figured that wasn't it. "The drunk man who was going to trip and fall overboard and drown tomorrow no longer will."

"Cool," Kendra said.

"However, there are still plenty of futures in which similar mishaps like that happen later."

Kendra groaned and rolled her eyes. "So you're saying the girl hasn't learned her lesson?"

"Why would she?" Chronos shrugged. "Presumably she cares a lot more about what her father thinks than what you think."

"That idiot," Kendra grumbled. "Maybe I *should* just kill her magical girl form."

"NO!" Chronos shouted.

"One magical girl form to save human lives. She'd still be alive, just unmagical. It's an acceptable tradeoff, oracle."

"And what would you do if she became a magical girl *again?*" Chronos demanded.

Kendra paused. "You think that's likely?"

"She isn't corrupt," Chronos said. "She's highly pressured by her circumstances to use magic constantly. She's younger than you were when you became a magical girl. I think it's highly likely she'll just keep becoming a magical girl over and over again, with the same powers every time."

Kendra groaned. In other words, the only way to prevent that was to kill the girl's human life, which wasn't something Kendra was willing to do. Even if they tried to take her prisoner, she'd just gain magic again and escape.

"Okay," Kendra grumbled. "What do you suggest?"

"Hmmmm . . ." Chronos looked at her hands and pondered. "This one might require a long-term touch . . ."

Chapter 2
The Serendipity

Xanthine yellow gumballs rolled between Dulcina's fingers as she listened to the interminable news reports from the various girls at the Magical Girl Union meeting.

"Elaine of Avalon says she won't join us," Golden Tingle Spray was saying. "She heard a rumor that the French Capitalist League is backing us. That isn't true, is it?"

"Of course not," Jeanne d'Rouen said scornfully. "We have the same rumor in France, only it's people saying that about the British Marxist League. Which is obvious nonsense. Marxists don't have any money. They're too busy giving it away to every whining mascot that comes along."

"Hey!" Golden Tingle Spray yelled. "At least that's better than being a bunch of selfish jerks who think they're better than everyone else!"

Florence looked weary.

Dulcina just shook her head. That silly quarrel between the two girls was now coming up at every meeting. It was a waste of time. As far as she was concerned, the answer was obvious: if a mascot asked for help, a magical girl should give it, and if not, she ought to be focusing on the problems in her own neighborhood instead. There was no reason to refuse or seek out mascots.

Golden Tingle Spray's insistence that there needed to be laws to force magical girls to help mascots when there were a lot going home unaided was silly. So was Jeanne d'Rouen's rebuttal that magical girls aiding mascots tended to be at higher risk of dying than magical girls who didn't.

As far as Dulcina was concerned, they were both completely missing the point.

First, mortality rate didn't matter. If one was more worried about her own life than helping others, she didn't deserve to be a magical girl in the first place.

And second, begrudging help was no help at all.

Florence's suggestion of creating a TV show to showcase the plight of specific mascots who needed help the most and weren't getting it, while also talking about the risks a magical girl might face if helping them, had seemed like an excellent idea to Dulcina. But both Golden Tingle Spray and Jeanne d'Rouen had objected loudly that it would help the other girl's cause more than her own.

After a few more minutes of quarreling, Golden Tingle Spray finally finished off her report, and it was Mellie's turn next.

Mellie was a new addition to the Magical Girl Union, replacing Bòidheach, who had quit a few weeks ago, shortly after the opening ceremonies. Unlike Tat'yana Tsvetok, the girl from Saint Petersburg who had quit without warning, Bòidheach had been open about her reason why: *"I hear you're instituting UNIFORMS! That goes against the whole point of being magical girls!"*

Despite Florence's befuddled insistence that there was no such plan, and she completely agreed that it would be idiotic, nothing had mollified the crimson-haired Scottish girl, and she'd sent in a rude and angry official resignation a few days later.

Mellie was a minor magical girl actress from Melbourne, not nearly as well-known or admired as the internationally famous Scottish model, but so far, Dulcina found her to be a much better addition to their meetings. She tended to listen calmly and give considered opinions, rather than spending half the meeting looking at her own reflection in a mirror admiringly.

Dulcina had not been fond of Bòidheach.

Mellie cleared her throat and spoke at a measured pace. "I've gotten the license for us to set up an office in Melbourne, and two of my friends are willing to help run it. I've also spoken with my director about the possibility of the mascot show, and he said he isn't very familiar with documentaries, but he'll see if there are any producers he knows who might be interested. He recommended seeing if we can get a grant from the Australian Mascot Bureau to produce the pilot episode."

"Nobody's going to watch an Australian show in Britain," Golden Tingle Spray said in a prickly voice.

"Well, we'll definitely watch it in Tarc!" Snowbelle declared, slapping her hands on the table and grinning. "Say, did you know I trained a girl once who had a snowflake as a mascot? It's true! A living snowflake! It couldn't even go inside. It would melt."

"Um . . ." Mellie looked taken aback. "Okay. So, I asked how much it would cost to run an ad for the Union during my show, and I got given this pricing chart . . ."

Dulcina eyed the Antarctican girl thoughtfully. Though she often came across like a shallow ditz, Snowbelle only ever seemed to interrupt with a non sequitur at a moment that would forestall an argument. She was starting to be impressed by the effectiveness of the girl's seemingly random sense of timing.

Next it was Asiyah Azhaar's turn. Eyes averted, she spoke with cautious slowness about the need for all the magical girls in the Union to take a brand new set of pictures with, um, rather more skin covered than most of the girls currently had before she could present the educational pamphlet in her country.

"They need to get over themselves," Princesa objected. "It's not like any of us look skanky, and these are our costumes!"

"You *would* say that," Delicate Frost Princess snorted. "You're the only one whose outfit's sleeveless."

"Um . . ." Asiyah Azhaar looked really uncomfortable. "They objected to yours even more . . ."

"What?!" Delicate Frost Princess exploded. "*Why?*"

"Well . . . um . . . the skirt's really short . . ."

"It's an ice-skating outfit!"

"That's it!" Snowbelle leapt up and slammed her hands on the table, eyes wide with excitement.

Most of the girls jumped, startled.

". . . What's it, Snowbelle?" Mellie asked cautiously.

"I've got the best idea for a jingle in Ireland!" Snowbelle cried, jumping up and down and waving her hands. "Just listen: 'Top o' the morning, little lassie! We'll help you be more cute and classy!'"

Cringes shot across the room.

"Because we need more recruitment in Great Britain, right?!" Snowbelle went on, orange curls bouncing as she leaned forward and put her hands on the table. "It's perfect!"

"Um . . . Snowbelle . . ." Florence said awkwardly, "the problem isn't getting more commercials in Britain. The problem is that our supporters there keep *backing out.*"

Golden Tingle Spray raised her hand. "Actually, about that — I have a theory. Do you think it could be because of that rumor that the French Capitalist League is secretly funding us? I don't know how it started, but a lot of people in London are saying it, and that's why Elaine of Avalon said she didn't want to join . . ."

"Actually, there's a rumor in Melbourne, too," Mellie said slowly. "Something about us favoring Brazil's interests over Australia's because we're in Mágico. One of my costars keeps telling me that and insisting it's true."

Delicate Frost Princess tapped her cheek, looking thoughtful. "Come to think of it, there's a rumor my friends in Frost City keep bringing up . . ."

"Mine, too," said Fecskefarkú Lepke.

"M-mine, too . . ." Météore murmured, looking down.

Voices raised to a babble as other girls spoke up at once.

Snowbelle rose her arms and waved them wildly. "What is this, a war of rumors?! Someone's out to sabotage us!"

Panicked looks flew around the table.

Dulcina stared at the Antarctican girl in puzzlement. *Why would you say that? Don't you usually calm people down?*

"Oh, I'm sure it's not that bad!" Asiyah Azhaar cried, holding out her hands in front of her. "I'm sure nobody would be that nasty!"

Namikaze Tateru and Chin-Sun exchanged knowing looks.

"Some might." Xinghuo spoke in a calm, even voice. "There are those who oppose our political ascendancy. It is just like those who spread lies about the *tianlong* because they have opposing agendas."

Namikaze Tateru snorted loudly.

Xinghuo ignored this. "Gossip is a common tactic of the malicious who don't want their identities known. If there are many rumors causing harm in many places, none of which have a grain of truth, it is likely not a coincidence."

Snowbelle slapped her hand on the table. "That explains it! My manager told me I ought to quit the Union if Mágico supports Brazilian expansion into Tarc. I wondered where he'd gotten that crazy idea from!"

"Hey, that's the rumor I heard, too!" Delicate Frost Princess exclaimed. "I heard magies from here wanted to buy Chill City."

"And obviously it isn't true," Snowbelle said, rolling her eyes. "We'd be the first to know if it was!"

Météore said awkwardly, "I've t-told m-my aunt it w-would b-be silly for the Union to t-take sides b-between B-Britain and France, b-but she d-didn't b-believe me."

"Yeah, like my mom," Schönwasser said, putting her face in her hands. "She keeps saying that if it's not true that the Union wants to move the Sönnig Exhibit of the Deutsches Museum to Mágico, then why does she keep hearing it?"

"My dad," Jeanne d'Rouen put in, nodding. "He says the same thing about the rumor with the British Marxist League."

"Oh, my gosh!" Golden Tingle Spray burst out. "You have no idea how annoying my aunt can be!"

At the head of the table, Florence took a deep breath. "Okay, quick question. How many of you have someone in your life who started begging you to leave the Union after hearing rumors?"

Hands raised all over the table. The only hands that didn't raise belonged to Chin-Sun, Namikaze Tateru, and Dulcina.

Interesting, Dulcina noted. *We are the only ones who have no social relationships. I have no personal life, and they reside in Mágico, away from friends or family.*

That meant that any girl who *could* be under attack from a rumor currently was.

Florence seemed to have come to the same conclusion. Her head was in her arms, and she was murmuring something Dulcina couldn't catch.

Chin-Sun picked up a long spear from beside her chair and placed it on the table in a troublingly offhanded manner. "So this is not mere coincidence. One of us has been sabotaging the rest."

Florence's head shot up. "Wait! How did you come to that conclusion?!"

"All of those rumors are regarding issues that were raised in this room at some point and discarded," Chin-Sun said. "I find it hard to believe that the person inventing them has not been privy to the information in our meetings."

That was a good point. It was a *disturbing* point.

"Th-that's easy to t-test," Météore said quickly. "I can t-tell if people are lying. Let's h-have everybody tell me whether they've sp-pread any rumors about the Union!"

Paranoid and wary looks flitted around the room.

"Good idea," Florence said firmly. "I don't think any of us are guilty, so we all have nothing to hide. I'll start. Météore, I have never spread any negative rumors about the Union, nor to my knowledge spread any false information about the Union. Am I telling the truth?"

Looking relieved, the shy French girl nodded.

"I'll go next," Xinghuo said briskly. "Since joining the Union, I have never said anything negative about it in anything other than in official and approved channels."

Météore nodded.

"I have not spread any rumors about the Magical Girl Union," Chin-Sun said in her usual monotone.

Météore nodded.

"I've spread a few lies, but only good ones to drive recruitment," Namikaze Tateru said, with a glint in her eye.

"Namikaze, please don't do that," Florence said, rubbing the side of her face. "We don't need lies to drive recruitment."

"W-well, she was t-telling the t-truth," Météore said.

The turn to be judged went around the table, one at a time. Delicate Frost Princess, Golden Tingle Spray, Fecskefarkú Lepke, and Schönwasser all wound up having to admit that they had sometimes badmouthed the Union to their friends, but they hadn't deliberately started any rumors.

Finally, everybody was exonerated.

When the last girl had spoken and judged to be telling the truth, Florence drew in a deep breath and let it out, belying her previous firm statement that she hadn't thought anyone was guilty.

Silence reigned across the table.

"It's probably a born mage," Delicate Frost Princess put in. "Maybe a villain with long-range hearing powers eavesdropping on us. That must be how they know what we've said."

Princesa drew in an angry breath.

"Or maybe it's a Deathwave minion with access to some kind of technology from another world!" Snowbelle babbled excitedly. "Or a villain from a totally different world!"

"Or maybe it's an organization without magic who's just very good at spying on us," Florence said flatly.

"Or maybe it's an organization without magic who's just very good at spying on us," Florence said flatly. "All we're doing right now is speculating, and I'd rather find the culprit. So, we need an investigation team. Anyone who's on it can be exempt from other duties until the culprits are found, and I'll reassign their duties between everyone else remaining."

Schönwasser leapt to her feet before she even finished talking. "Ooh! Let me help! I have tracking powers!"

"I c-can t-tell if p-people are lying . . ." Météore said shyly.

"I don't sleep," Dulcina added. She didn't mind the idea of being exempt from these meetings.

"Great," Florence said, nodding curtly. "You three can start looking into it. In the meantime, I want to talk about this 'volunteer accountants' thing we've been doing. I went through last month's statements and found no fewer than twelve basic math errors . . ."

Dulcina went back to rolling the yellow gumballs from her sandals between her fingers, smiling in satisfaction. Being part of this investigation team would save her a lot of time. Time she could spend doing more patrolling of Mexico City.

"ARGH!!" Rhea shouted, leaping to her feet and clenching her fists.

Heracles looked up from his mound of paperwork nervously. "Boss? What's wrong?"

"Those Magical Girl Union girls figured it out *much* too quickly!" Rhea ranted, slamming herself back into her seat. "They didn't even bother to fall for my trap of making it look like one of them was responsible! I *hate* truth-telling powers!"

Minerva had been skeptical that their ideal outcome would happen, because truth magic was such an annoying power. But Rhea had optimistically assumed that since Météore wasn't being deliberately lied to, they'd be able to drive her out of the Union before they started Phase Two.

The fact that her minion's skepticism had been well-founded did not put Rhea in a good temper.

Of course she had an alternate plan. She had hundreds of them. But she'd really wanted to drive Météore, Xinghuo, and Snowbelle out of the Union before anybody caught on to the fact that the rumors were a deliberate war.

All of them would be hard to manipulate in person.

Météore could tell if people were lying.

Xinghuo could sense sincerity.

Snowbelle seemed to possess an instinctive sense for knowing when tension was brewing, leaping in with a random comment to defuse the situation. She also had a way of making people trust her and follow her, which was impossibly aggravating when you were trying to sow seeds of dissension and distrust.

Still . . . the two girls the rumors *had* driven out of the Union so far were huge victories. Tat'yana Tsvetok would have been a tremendous nuisance, and Bòidheach was a terrific ally.

Not that Bòidheach had any idea she was Rhea's ally. She simply had a tendency to become passionately hateful towards anything she quit, so she was already pushing the rumors far and wide and lending them more legitimacy. It was highly amusing.

Meanwhile, Tat'yana Tsvetok's power to sense morality would have been the worst possible threat for Rhea to face. Xinghuo and Météore she could fool in person if she had to, but the Russian girl who literally saw good and evil?

No, the only option would have been to send Drake to kill her, both human life and magical girl form, and while Rhea wouldn't have minded ridding the world of that pest in the least, it would have made it far more difficult to lure the rest of the girls into a sense of security.

Fortunately, Tat'yana Tsvetok had barely needed a tiny push. She had joined the Union because she'd trusted both Florence and Snowbelle, but when she'd met some of the other girls, she had been instantly uncomfortable.

Rhea had, quite naturally, gone over Tat'yana Tsvetok's reactions to the other girls many times to figure out which ones would be the easiest to push into corruption first.

Golden Tingle Spray, Namikaze Tateru, Dulcina Caramelo, and Bòidheach had made the Russian girl extremely uncomfortable. Naturally, this was why Bòidheach had come to Rhea's attention and become her second target.

Jeanne d'Rouen, Schönwasser, Edelweiss, and Xinghuo had all made her moderately uncomfortable, which meant they might be corruptible if Rhea did it slowly and carefully.

She had been only slightly uncomfortable around Delicate Frost Princess, Météore, Fecskefarkú Lepke, Eloise Santos, and Chin-Sun — the last one a disappointing surprise for Rhea, because she'd had high hopes for an emotionless spy.

And Tat'yana Tsvetok had seemed perfectly at ease around Florence, Asiyah Azhaar, La Rama Fragrante, and Snowbelle, so Rhea would probably have to have them all killed eventually.

Of course, while the Russian girl's initial reactions had been useful, Rhea couldn't have risked letting her stay.

So the first place she had sent Minerva to spread rumors had been Saint Petersburg, and the rumor had been that Namikaze Tateru was planning to use the Union as a front to gather allies to assassinate the Japanese emperor. It wasn't a very creative rumor, given that it was approximately half true, but it had worked like a charm.

Two days after hearing it from her sister, Tat'yana Tsvetok had sent a message to Florence, quitting the Union without explanation. And Rhea had already selected her replacement.

Having noticed that Florence had mentioned Princesa as a possible recruit at one point, and knowing that Princesa was both a controversial figure and a born mage with a prickly temper, Rhea had been only too happy to send Minerva to spread rumors in Peru that the Magical Girl Union was a front for born mages who wanted to encourage more of them to become magical girls.

This had had exactly the intended double effect: Princesa had immediately volunteered to join the Union, at a time when Florence had been desperate to find a replacement for Tat'yana Tsvetok before the opening ceremonies, and many other Peruvian magical girls had been left soured about the idea of the Union.

As for the replacement for Bòidheach, the glowing rumors Rhea had spread through France had not been able to convince Météore or Jeanne d'Rouen to recommend recruiting Belle Mode, a popular Parisian magical girl who was secretly obsessed with the fashionable dark form Rhea had designed for her, but Rhea's rumors *had* at least successfully blocked Khwām Mettā, a Thai pacifist, from joining.

It had been close, too. The Thai magical girl had nearly said yes. She and Asiyah Azhaar had gotten along famously, a bad sign if Rhea ever saw one.

In the end, the Union had recruited Mellie, not a fantastic choice from Rhea's point of view, but not a complete disaster, either. She could probably manipulate that girl just fine, so there was no need to be in a rush to replace her.

Rhea stared at her hands and sighed moodily. *But is that it? Are those all the girls I'll be able to persuade to quit and replace?*

"Boss . . .?" Heracles asked, looking over worriedly.

"I wanted to have more than four weeks at this!" Rhea exploded, slamming her fist on the table. "I should have been able to lead them by the nose for at least another month. But no! That Snowbelle girl had to serendipitously come up with exactly the right answer, and now they're all fixated on it! She figured it out much too quickly!"

"Um . . . figured out what too quickly?" The fourteen-year-old minion in charge of paperwork looked lost. "Four weeks at what?"

". . . Nothing . . ." Rhea sighed, waving her hand for him to get back to work. *I miss having a competent minion with me.*

Well, throwing a fit wouldn't fix her plans that were now torn to ribbons. She would have to readjust and see what she could do with the members of the Magical Girl Union board of directors who were probably now going to stay in place.

Princesa was a good place to start.

Chapter 3
The Misfortune

Just as Amy was flipping a page of her book, the door slammed.

Daddy stormed into their hotel room, flinging his coat on the ground. "That stupid villain!"

Amy looked up timidly from her book. "What's she done this time, Daddy?"

"She's warned another casino about how your power works and what my name is, that's what! She's *warned* them!"

Amy cringed. She didn't quite dare say, *Why are you surprised, Daddy? She's been doing that for two weeks. She always seems to know exactly where you're going to try next.*

She definitely didn't dare say, *Maybe you could get a job and I could go back to school again.*

But maybe he would think of it himself. There seemed to be no end to the casino-warning in sight. They could get in the car, drive sixteen hours without stopping, and get out at the first casino they saw, and somehow, the villain woman would always have been there only two hours ago.

At some point, Daddy would realize that they had to get money somehow and he couldn't do that by gambling, right?

At some point, Daddy would realize that they were down to their last two hundred dollars, right?

At some point, Daddy would realize the only thing left to do was to be sensible, right?

"I'm sorry, Daddy —" Amy began.

"That's the thirteenth casino in two weeks!" he exploded. "*Thirteen!*"

Amy stiffened. *Has it been exactly thirteen?*

That was the unluckiest number, a bad omen. If you didn't notice a thirteen, sometimes you were safe. But if you ever saw one, it meant something bad was about to happen.

"They all say I've been cheating!" Daddy sputtered, furious. "I haven't been *cheating!*"

Amy gulped and looked away. She had to say something before the thirteen kicked in. "W-well . . . Daddy . . . technically magic *is* considered cheating . . . I mean, it's in the rules and everything. Like card-counting . . ."

Daddy brushed that away with a wave of his hand. "If they can't tell you're doing it, it doesn't count as cheating."

Amy wasn't sure she agreed, but she didn't want to argue. Especially not with a thirteen looming. Someone wasn't going to break in here and steal their last few dollars, were they?

Her father sat down in a chair, pulled out a cigarette, and lit it, saying flatly, "There's nothing for it, Amy: you're going to have to fight her."

Amy's panic skyrocketed. "M-me?!"

"Of course you," her father snorted, taking a deep draw from his cigarette. "You're the one with the magic, aren't you?"

Amy flung her arms out in desperation. "I'm not a fighter, Daddy!!"

He exhaled a large cloud of smoke. "Sure you are. You can do that bad luck thing, can't you?"

"That's not a power! That's a *cost!*"

"Power or cost, I don't care. Just kill the villain."

Amy stared at him in horror. *Did he just . . .? Did he just . . .?*

Had Daddy just asked her to *kill* somebody?!

"And if that doesn't work, we'll hire you out," her father said, putting out his cigarette on the no-smoking sign.

Amy stared at him. "Hire me . . . out?"

"Well, I assume your power can work for other gamblers, not just me," her father said matter-of-factly, removing his shoes and tossing them across the room. "It wouldn't be any fun, but we have to do what we have to. I figure you could help out a good two or three people a night without anyone noticing, and we'd take a cut of the profits."

Amy stared at him in horror. *Two or three people a night?!*

Did he have any idea how much luck that would take? Not only to make several people lucky in the same room at once, but also to make sure none of them would be stupid enough to get caught and give her away?

If the casino owners knew she was there, and they knew she could manipulate the odds without their being able to sense it, some of them might decide to kill her. And even if they didn't, her father might wind up in prison, and she might wind up in juvenile detention! Luck wouldn't help her there!

Not to mention that if word got out what her power could do, she might get kidnapped and held for ransom, and kept forever and forced to help a criminal rob banks or something.

Nothing good would happen if Daddy did that! This was the worst thirteen in the world!

But killing somebody . . .

Killing somebody . . .

"It's not safe," she pleaded. "I could get hurt, Daddy."

He brushed that off. "Don't be a coward. You don't need safety: you're *lucky*. You'll win."

Tears welled up in her eyes. "But . . . I don't want to hurt anybody . . ."

"Whine whine whine," her father snorted, reaching into his pocket for a new cigarette. He found one and lit it, then looked over at her with exasperation. "Just go get ready. You're going to kill the villain tonight."

Amy blinked back tears. She couldn't think of a single way out of this.

Why couldn't the villain have stopped before thirteen?

"Welcome, Seraph," said a nasally magical voice.

Chronos looked up to see Kendra descending the staircase. She glanced over to the side of the room to see Tiffany pushing a button on her voice synthesizer with an eager look on her face.

Kendra had scarcely bothered to acknowledge the existence of their third teammate since the incident in England. It was starting to worry Chronos.

"Hi, Kendra," Chronos said.

"Welcome, Seraph," put in the voice.

"Hi, oracle. Hi, Tiffany," Kendra said coolly, looking directly at Chronos and not turning her head an inch.

Chronos sighed. It seemed tonight was not going to be the night the stubborn former magical girl stopped giving Tiffany the close-to-silent treatment.

"Are you finished already?" Chronos asked.

Kendra shrugged. "Nothing too challenging."

"Why don't you tell me what you did on those missions?" Chronos asked suspiciously.

"All right. I've silenced Nightingale, knocked sense into that brainwashed girl in Madagascar, and stopped Blueberry Yoghurt. Now which casino am I hitting today?"

Chronos quickly flicked through all three of those magical girls' futures. To her exasperation, Kendra seemed to have broken the focus item of the brainwashed magical girl.

"You do realize it wasn't Magie Mignonne's *fault* that she was attacking her friends, right?" Chronos asked indignantly, holding up her hands to show the girl creating a new focus item.

Kendra shrugged. "And?"

"And you could have knocked some sense into her in some other way!"

"It wasn't an heirloom focus item, oracle. She can make another one that's exactly the same. In fact, it looks like she's about to."

Chronos slapped her hands shut. "That's not the point!"

"Really? What is the point?"

"The point is, you keep on doing things that are too extreme to solve the problem!"

Kendra yawned. "Oracle, you really need to get some combat experience before you judge the way I handle everything."

A gleam rose in her eye.

"Actually . . ."

"No!" Chronos said immediately. "You'd be amazed to find how much better I'd be than Tiffany at betraying you on a battlefield if you tried to force me to join you."

Kendra looked disappointed.

"Welcome, Seraph," the synthesized voice put in.

Kendra didn't react a smidge. "Well? Which casino do I go to tonight?"

Chronos wasn't willing to let the subject go. "How would *you* have felt if, instead of showing you your future, I'd just teleported in and broken your focus item without warning?"

"That's not what happened, oracle." Kendra rolled her eyes. "And as for that, what makes you think you could have? I'd have killed you first."

"All arrogance aside," Chronos snorted, "how would you have felt?"

Kendra considered that for half a second. "Annoyed. Then I'd have made another focus item and killed you with it."

Chronos shook her head in exasperation. Appeals to empathy, it seemed, were lost on Kendra.

"Welcome, Seraph. Welcome, Seraph. Welcome, Seraph."

Kendra folded her arms and didn't look over at Tiffany. "So, which casino? I assume he'll try a new one tonight."

"Er . . ." Chronos glanced down at her hands. "You, um . . . you might not want to go to any. Marina Amethyst seems to be planning to stop you."

"Ha!" Kendra smirked, waving a hand in amusement. "How would she even know where to find me?"

"*Luck powers,* Kendra?" Chronos said in exasperation. "There's a 90% chance she'll be at any casino you pick."

"Welcome, Seraph. Welcome, Seraph. Welcome, Seraph."

"Sheesh, you'd think she'd be grateful," Kendra said, shaking her head. "I've stopped her dad from gambling, haven't I?"

"Welcome, Seraph. Welcome, Seraph. Welcome, Seraph."

"Yes, you've definitely broken his addiction and made sure she never has to worry about being asked to use her power again," Chronos said dryly. "I'm sure she appreciates how sustainable and long-term this solution is."

Kendra put her hands on her hips. "*You're* the one who had the idea! If you want me to do something else, just say so!"

Chronos hesitated. Figuring out how to push someone in a particular direction wasn't exactly her strong point. She preferred to just leave other people alone and in turn be left alone.

"Maybe you could try telling him his daughter depends on him to straighten out?" Chronos hazarded.

Kendra snorted. "I'm sure that would work so much better."

"Well, *you* come up with a better idea!"

"Okay." Kendra shrugged. "I'll go to the casino and meet with Marina Amethyst."

"I said a better idea, not a worse one!"

Kendra smirked. "Don't doubt me, soothsayer. I'm good at my work."

Chronos stared at her suspiciously. "And by that, you mean killing magical girl forms?"

"Only when it's necessary."

"It's *never* necessary!"

"If you joined me in combat sometimes, you'd know that it is."

"Welcome, Seraph. Welcome, Seraph."

"And Tiffany, would you turn off that stupid voice synthesizer?!" Kendra shouted, finally losing her temper and whirling around.

Tiffany giggled, looking delighted to have gotten a reaction. "Victor the Voice Synthesizer has the hiccups! That's why he keeps repeating himself! Listen!"

She jabbed the button again and again.

"Welcome, Seraph. Welcome, Seraph. Welcome, Seraph. Welcome, Seraph."

"TIFFANY . . .!"

"Hee hee!"

"Okay, I'm off," Kendra said, spinning around. "Unless there's anyone else I need to stop first?"

"No, I think you've got everyb—"

"Welcome, Seraph. Welcome, Seraph. Welcome, Seraph. Welcome, Seraph."

Kendra had already teleported out.

"Tiffany," Chronos said, looking over at the young girl, "why don't you take that toy somewhere else?"

"But Victor likes being here," Tiffany said earnestly.

"Why don't you take *yourself* somewhere else?"

"I like being here, too!"

"Maybe you could like being upstairs, instead."

"No, I like being downstairs!"

Chronos sighed, heaved herself out of her chair, and headed up to her room.

Chapter 4
The Jinx

Unlucky symbols hung across Amy's belt as she waited, her heart pounding.

It seemed to be beating out two different phrases at once.

Don't show up. Don't show up. Don't show up.

Please show up. Please show up. Please show up.

If the woman showed up, Amy would have to make her so unlucky that she might die.

If the woman *didn't* show up, things might be even worse.

The woman appeared in a cloud of sparkles.

"Marina Amethyst!" Amy whispered in a panic, crossing her fingers over her head for some desperately-needed luck.

Something weird happened. The four-leaf clover spun around in a blur and turned into a long, thin U-shape. The moment Amy hopped through it, it tilted upside down, and her clothes looked different from usual.

Instead of pale and forest green, her dress was now emerald with hunter green and yellow highlights. Instead of stockings, she now wore sandals with a four-leaf clover on each. When she touched her ears, she felt a pair of earrings that were U-shaped and upside down. And across a thin yellow belt were all the unlucky symbols she had brought, just in case.

Amy's heart pounded. *What's going on? I don't understand.*

She glanced over her shoulder at her four-leaf clover, which was still a giant, upside-down U. It spun in a circle rapidly, then shrank and zoomed into a rightside-up tiny horseshoe to the right of her neckline.

Something's different! Amy wanted to scream. *What happened to my four-leaf clover?!*

The villain woman kept on walking towards the entrance to the casino. Amy had to do something, fast.

She reached for the magical dice she often handed to her father before they went into a casino, but there were no pockets in her new skirt. The dice were gone.

Amy panicked. Why had her outfit changed? Was it a power-up? How was she going to fight the villain?

"Things can't get worse!" Amy shouted, pointing her left arm forward and clenching her other hand into a fist behind her.

The curse slammed into the villain, sending her flying against a wall to the left of the entrance.

"Wow," the villain woman said, getting up and rubbing her head. "You *changed your magical girl form* for your dad? He must be so proud."

"It's not his fault! This is all your fault!" Amy yelled, clenching her fists. "You're the reason it changed! If I can't stop you, Daddy wants to hire me out to *other* gamblers for money!!"

"And?" the woman asked, shrugging.

"And what?!" Amy shrieked, on the edge of hysteria.

"And you would just let him?"

"I wouldn't have a choice!"

"You need to seriously work on your 'no'-saying skills."

Amy seized an unlucky object from her belt. She couldn't think of anything else to do.

"Lucky rabbit's foot . . ."

She flung it forward with all her strength.

"UNLUCKY RABBIT!"

With inhuman reflexes, the woman ducked, and it sailed over her head.

Amy stared at her, mute. "...ducked..."

The woman smirked, folding her arms. "Got anything else?"

Filled with determination, Amy reached for the tiny bag hanging at her waist. It held a penny. Pennies could go either way. Heads would make you lucky enough to find other coins, and tails would make you unlucky enough to drop some.

She pulled the penny out and dropped it on the ground. It rolled around and landed on heads.

Not what she was looking for, but she could use that to make herself lucky.

Amy leaned over and scooped it up. As she tossed it in the air, she chanted the rhyme she always said: "Find a penny, pick it up; all day long, you'll get good luck." As the penny arced upward: "Heads!"

A bladed ring swung through and sliced the penny in half.

Both halves missed her hand, falling to the ground and dinging gently against the pavement.

Amy stared at the villain, open-mouthed.

"See ya." The woman shrugged and headed back for the casino entrance.

"No! Come back here!" Amy cried frantically. She caught sight of a bad luck symbol skulking across the street and crossed her fingers in front of her to summon it. *"Black cat!"*

"Meowwwww!" A furious black cat whooshed through the air in front of the villain. It landed in a pile of garbage on the other end of the alley, picked itself up, and then bolted away.

The villain folded her arms, looking unimpressed. "Well, now that you've molested the local wildlife, can you go home?"

Amy looked around frantically for a ladder, but there was no sign of any such thing here. She reached for the upside-down horseshoe on her belt —

"Are you *trying* to make me get serious?" the villain inquired, looking mildly annoyed. "You know I could kill you if I wanted to, right?"

Amy froze.

"'Kay, thanks, bye," the villain said, heading back to the door.

"I just want you to LEAVE MY DAD *ALONE!*" Amy shrieked.

"Yeah, so you can keep cursing bad luck on random people?" The villain snorted, turning around. "Not happening. Why did you even design your power that way?"

Amy clenched her fists. Why didn't the villain woman understand how luck worked? *"I have no choice!!"*

The villain stared at her flatly for a moment. Then she waved a hand and summoned a bladed ring. "All right. Killing your magical girl form it is."

Amy yelped and grabbed the upside-down horseshoe from her belt, meaning to aim it at the villain. But she missed and aimed it at herself. She collapsed to the ground, covering her head with her empty hand and cowering.

Something whooshed towards her, but Amy's right arm seemed to move on its own, wildly swinging the horseshoe in every direction.

Crash!

Wham!

Clang!

Amy peeked up, her heart hammering.

The villain was holding her bladed ring weapon and standing over Amy, looking annoyed.

"Wh-what happened?" Amy ventured.

"You deflected it. Over and over again."

"H-how'd I do that?"

The villain snorted derisively.

Amy breathed in deeply. Did that mean she was . . . safe? Was she so lucky that the villain couldn't hurt her? Did she have magic that would protect her from getting hit, no matter what?

Or had the black cat made the villain unlucky?

Or was it both?

"M-maybe I should just become a fighter!" Amy exclaimed as realization struck her. *This* had to be the reason her magical girl form had changed! "Funnel all of Daddy's bad luck into fighting villains instead! Then that wouldn't hurt anybody except people who deserved it . . ."

The villain woman's face softened.

"Yeah, maybe," she said softly, looking pitying. "That's what I would do if I were you. But I'm not sure I'm a good role model."

Amy swallowed. "B-but it's perfect. Daddy will be happy, I won't have to be unhappy, and . . ."

"Really? Were you happy before?" the villain queried.

Amy fell silent.

"'Cause here's what I think," the woman wearing black said relentlessly. "I think your lucky power would've kept Chronos from noticing you, just like everybody else, unless you *wanted* someone who was capable of stopping you to do so. Then my showing up would've been lucky for you."

Amy's eyes filled with tears. "N-not everybody fails to notice me. Luck doesn't always work . . ."

"Yeah, but I bet it usually does." The villain shrugged wryly. "Look at this. Nobody in the casino has even noticed our fight and come out here to check it out. Why not? I'm an obvious villain. They'd all be on the side of the sweet-looking magical girl. That would be entirely to your advantage. Unless what's *actually* to your advantage is hearing me talk."

Amy was silent. She looked down at the horseshoe, larger than it had been on her belt and rightside-up in her hands.

Why had her four-leaf clover become a horseshoe?

Why had the only thing in the world that was all good luck turned into something that could be both good luck and bad?

"I won't stop you if you wanna use your bad luck power to fight villains," the woman in black said. "That seems reasonable enough. But think about it. Do you really want your magical girl form — the deepest manifestation of who you are — to be all about your dad?"

Tears welled up in Amy's eyes. *It's ALWAYS been all about my dad!*

Except it hadn't. For a few glorious weeks before her father had figured out she had magic, she'd used her magic to play.

For a few glorious weeks, Marina Amethyst had been the one good thing in a life without their house. Without their car. Without her school. Without Mummy.

"But if it would make Daddy happy . . ." Amy said faintly.

"Has your magic made him happy so far, or has it just made his gambling habit worse?" the villain demanded.

Amy faltered. "B-both, I guess . . ."

"Has it ever made him satisfied? *Ever?*"

". . . N-no . . ."

"So whether you help him or not really makes no difference," the villain said cruelly. "No matter what, he'll just keep gambling your life away, and you'll never get to be happy."

Amy choked back a sob.

"Not to mention that he'd still be gambling long after you outgrew your powers." The villain turned away from her and headed towards the casino entrance. "Think about it."

Amy didn't try to stop her. She just sat there, swallowing.

As the villain barged into the casino, Amy pulled the mirror compact off her belt and stared into her own reflection.

Why had she brought a mirror, the most unlucky thing in the world?

Why hadn't she thought to use it on the villain woman, even for a moment?

Amy hadn't looked closely in a mirror for seven years now. She was too scared of them. Her eyes looked so sad . . .

Seven years . . .

Amy sat up straight, a gasp catching in her throat.

It had been seven years since she'd broken the mirror. Seven years exactly on the day before the woman in the black costume with buckles had shown up the first time.

The villain woman was right. It hadn't been Amy's good luck keeping people from noticing her and stopping her father. It had been Amy's *bad* luck.

But now the curse from the mirror was over.

She could do something different.

She *should* do something different.

Amy stood, shutting the mirror compact and slipping it back on her belt. She knew why she had brought a mirror, and it hadn't been to stop the villain. She didn't care about the villain.

She'd changed her magical girl form because she didn't want to be a lucky charm anymore.

She wanted to be a jinx.

Deep in the depth of night, a man was gambling at a casino, laughing raucously.

A girl in shining emerald green walked out of the bathroom with an enormous oval-shaped mirror, grunting and straining as she carried it behind her.

Immediately recognizing her as a magical girl, twelve gamblers from tables converged on her in a fever of excitement, accusation, and greed, but she only muttered, "Tails!" and a slot machine started shooting out coins in wild directions. The people screamed and scrambled to grab as many as they could.

Two bouncers moved forward from the exit, but she muttered, "Black cat!" and a furious cat exploded from a trash can where she'd trapped it, leaping at the momentarily panicked bouncers, hissing and clawing and distracting them for precious seconds.

Guns were aimed at her and jammed. Somebody rushed to stop her and tripped and fell.

She stopped behind a man with a stack of poker chips beside him and a rapturous look on his face.

"Seven years' bad luck!!" she shouted.

The mirror shattered, slivers and chunks cascading all over the floor.

"*What the —?!*" The man leapt up from his seat, seeing the magical girl behind him. "Amy?! What'd you do to your dress?!"

"Now you have to *stop gambling!*" the girl shouted, her voice high-pitched with discomfort and determination. "You won't be able to win again until I'm *eighteen!*"

"What're you talking about?!" the man hollered, his face turning red. "You can't do any such thing!"

"Can so!" the girl yelled. "It's my new magical girl power! I'm not a lucky charm anymore — I'm a jinx! I'll jinx you every time you try to gamble until I'm old enough to live on my own!"

"AMY!" the man shouted. "That's insane! Don't you dare!"

The bouncers grabbed the man's arms, holding them behind his back. Another member of security grabbed the magical girl's arms and did the same with them. She didn't try to protest as they were dragged unceremoniously out of the building and dumped on the pavement.

The man protested vehemently, shouting that he didn't know this girl and he was being framed for cheating, which he would never do, until the door slammed in his face.

He breathed heavily, staring lividly at his daughter. "Never do that again, Amy. Or else."

"Or else what?" she shot back, face red. "You're jinxed now. Even if you get rid of me, you won't be able to win a single game for seven years!"

The man's eyes blazed. He clenched a fist and raised it —

And someone chucked the black cat out of the casino, which landed, hissing and snarling, on the man's face. He screamed as the claws dug in and fought to get it away from him.

"We're g-going to go to Grandma's," the magical girl said, her face red and her voice starting to stumble. "Sh-she likes me better than you. If I tell her what we've b-been doing, she'll b-be furious. The o-only reason she didn't take me away before was that I told her I was h-happy with you. But I'm never going to lie or do magic to help you again! And if you try to guilt-trip me to do it again, I'm going to live with Grandma for good!"

The man was too busy fighting to get the cat off his face and cursing to say anything.

The girl sat on the pavement and waited until the cat fell to the ground, landed on all-fours, and darted off, still hissing.

"Could've done something about the cat, couldn't you?" the man snarled.

The magical girl swallowed several times and then shook her head. "No, Daddy. I can't give other people good luck anymore. I'm a jinx. That's all I am, and all I'll ever be, from now on."

The man stared at her in fury, and then turned and stormed off without a word.

The girl drew in a deep, ragged breath, seeming to be trying not to cry. She drew a tiny pouch from her belt and dropped a penny onto the ground.

"Find a penny, pick it up; all day long, you'll get good luck," she chanted, scooping it up. "Heads."

She headed down the pavement away from the casino, tears glistening down her face, often stopping to pick up another coin. When she had gathered several of the largest denomination, she stopped at a payphone and pushed them into the machine and dialed.

"Hello, Grandma?" the girl said in a small, shaky voice. "I need you to come pick me up."

Chronos dropped her hands down to the table and stared at them pensively.

"Huh . . ." she said.

That future was almost guaranteed to happen tomorrow. But there was still time to stop it. She could have Kendra intervene.

Yet . . . maybe it was better not to.

She'll be able to escape from being used for her magic while she's still a child, Chronos thought, flicking through the girl's many branching futures. Some of them were sad, but most of them were better than the futures she'd had before. *I'm . . . jealous.*

Chronos hadn't been able to escape from the Olympians, or from her sister Rhea, until adulthood.

Of course she didn't think tomorrow was the best future possible. She had no doubt the results of that choice wouldn't be what Amy Marin was hoping for. But she could understand how it might be necessary. And it seemed wrong to interfere when the girl had so clearly made up her mind.

If Chronos had been able to escape at the age of eleven, her life would probably have been much better.

"Well, that's a future we can live with, I guess," Chronos said quietly. "Good luck to you."

www.ingramcontent.com/pod-product-compliance
Lightning Source LLC
Chambersburg PA
CBHW022043050726
47591CB00003B/933